PUZZLE ISLAND

Contents

About this story

This story is about a young pirate called Sam Swashbuckle, his pet parrot, Percy, and their adventures on Puzzle Island.

Sam's new boat

Percy the parrot

Useful equipment

Sam Swashbuckle

Skull and crossbones badge

Sam is a junior pirate. To become a real pirate, he has to find a skull and crossbones badge, like the one shown on the left. The badge is hidden in a chest full of treasure and buried somewhere on Puzzle Island. An exciting trail of clues and puzzles will lead Sam to it.

Puzzle Island

Treasure chest

You will find a puzzle on every double page. See if you can solve them all and help Sam to follow the treasure trail. If you get stuck, you can look at the answers on pages 31 and 32.

The Pirate Kit

On his journey, Sam also collects a pirate kit. One piece of kit is hidden on every double page. See if you can spot the pieces as you go. If you can't find them all, the answers on page 32 should help you. Here you can see the complete pirate kit.

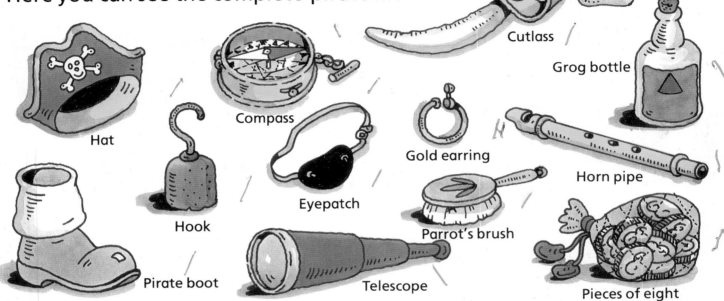

Spare headscarf

Be careful!

Cutlass

Grog bottle

Hat

Compass

Gold earring

Horn pipe

Hook

Eyepatch

Parrot's brush

Pirate boot

Telescope

Pieces of eight

Horatio

Horatio is a sneaky pirate who would love to beat Sam to the treasure on Puzzle Island. He is lurking on almost every double page. Keep your eyes open!

Horatio

HELGA

Horace, Horatio's pet snake

Pink Elephants

Puzzle Island is the home of the only pink elephants in the world. There is at least one pink elephant hiding on every double page. How many can you spot?

Now turn the page to begin the adventure...

3

Sam sets off

Early one morning Sam's adventure began. He was off on his treasure hunt. He waved goodbye to his mum and his dad, his granny and his little sister, and set sail for Puzzle Island in his new red boat.

The sun was shining and the sea was blue. It was a perfect day to look for treasure. But Sam knew he had to keep a special watch out for Horatio, the sneaky pirate. He was sure to be somewhere near.

Can you see Horatio?

Don't forget to look out for a piece of pirate kit — and those pink elephants!

Squawk squawk!

Bye!

4

5

Where is Puzzle Island?

Sam sailed and sailed, until he saw some strange islands ahead. Quickly he checked his sea chart.

"One of them must be Puzzle Island," he cried.

But which one was it? Sam remembered that Puzzle Island was the home of the only pink elephants in the world. If he could spot just one pink elephant, he would have found Puzzle Island.

Can you spot a pink elephant?

6

Remember to look out for Horatio, and a piece of pirate kit!

7

The first clue

Sam jumped off his boat, tripped and bumped his head on a large signpost. He was in luck! He had found his first clue.

Sam looked around. He saw lots of paths and lots of arrows. But where was the red and white stripy arrow that would start his treasure hunt?

Can you see it?

FIRST CLUE
Follow the
red and white
stripy arrow

8

Remember to look out for Horatio, and a piece of pirate kit, and the pink elephants. This is your last reminder!

9

The leafy lake

Sam sped off down the path. He was so excited he almost fell – splash – into a big lake. He tried to run around it, but he couldn't squeeze past the prickly branches.

The lake was covered with lots of giant leaves. Maybe Sam could use them as stepping stones to hop across the lake? But some of the leaves were animals' nests, and some of the leaves had holes in them. He mustn't hop on any of these.

Can you find a way across the lake by hopping from one leaf to another?

NESTING SEASON Do not disturb the baby animals

The safe bridge

Next he came to the edge of a high cliff. He gulped as he looked down. Far below he saw hungry crocodiles and strange animals, bubbling mud and whirling whirlpools.

Ten bridges crossed the gorge. Sam was about to step on to one of them when Percy squawked a warning. Sam looked again and saw that only one bridge was safe to cross.

Do you know which one it is?

Squawk!

Animal spotting

Safe on the other side, Sam saw a strange sight. A man peered down at him from a tall tower.

"I'm on a treasure trail and I don't know where to go next," Sam called. "Can you help me?"

"Yes, if you help me first," said the man. "I've spotted all the animals in my animal spotting book except for a lion, a tiger, a giraffe, a monkey, a snake and a spotty dog. Find me the animals and I'll show you the trail."

Can you spot all the animals?

The volcano maze

The old man told Sam to go to the red flag at the top of the volcano. There he would find something very useful. Sam looked at the maze of paths ahead of him. Would he ever make his way through them?

Can you find your way through the maze to the red flag at the top of the volcano?

Quick sands

Spot the difference

Sam followed the steep, winding path to the top of the volcano. There in the middle of the crater was a big silver key. It looked very useful, so Sam picked it up. Tied to it was a label which told him to go to the orchard. He put the key in his bag and set off at once.

When he reached the orchard, Sam thought he heard noises behind him. Was he being followed? Slowly he looked over his shoulder, but there was no one there.

"I hope I don't bump into Horatio," he shivered.

Suddenly there was a loud cracking noise. Sam spun around. How strange. He was sure there was someone else in the orchard, and several things looked different.

Can you spot the differences between the two pictures?

Find the twins

All of a sudden, Horatio leapt out from behind a tree. But before he could net poor Sam, he was startled by the sound of splashing and shouting. Nearby, children were playing on the beach.

   "Which way to the treasure?" Horatio asked them gruffly.

   Horatio looked very puzzled at the answers, but Sam smiled. He knew the way now.

Where should Sam go next?

Pyramid puzzle

Horatio sped off at once – towards the snake pit! Sam waited until he was out of sight and then ran to the pyramids. There were three of them, one yellow, one red and one blue.

Nailed to some trees, Sam saw four pieces of paper. Quickly he pulled them off and unrolled them. They were four maps of the area. But only one of them was right. This was the map that showed Sam where he would find the next clue.

You can see the maps on the next page. Which is the right map? Where is the next clue?

X marks the spot where the next clue is hidden.

23

Locked out!

There was a spiked wall all around the blue pyramid. It was much too high for Sam to climb, and the heavy gate was locked with a big padlock. Sam wondered what to do next. Was this the end of the trail?

Suddenly he had a brainwave. There was something in his back pack that would open the gate. Quickly he emptied his bag on the ground.

What can Sam use to open the gate?

The pirate's den

The lock opened with a click. Sam climbed the steps to a door in the pyramid and slowly pushed it open. He found himself in a pirate's den filled with all sorts of strange things.

There were six closed doors inside the den, and on each door there was a message and a picture. Five of the pictures showed places Sam had already been to on his journey around the island. But there was one picture he didn't recognize. This was where he had to go to next.

Which door should Sam go through?

Spies at the waterfall

Sam opened the door. He ran down the steps on the other side, through a door in the spiked wall he hadn't seen before, and along a path to the waterfall. On the ground was a cross. Was the treasure buried here?

Quickly he pulled out his spade and began to dig. Just then he heard rustling noises all around him. He was being watched, but he wasn't afraid. He knew the spies were friendly, because he had seen them all before.
How many people do you recognize?

The wonderful treasure!

Sam's spade hit something hard. It was the treasure chest! His friends cheered as Sam puffed and panted and heaved the heavy chest out of the ground. He opened the lid and gasped. Inside was the most wonderful treasure Sam had ever seen. There were glittering jewels and chocolate money, amazing toys and lots of toffees. Then Sam spotted the most important treasure of all. He was a real pirate at last!

Can you see what Sam has spotted?

Answers

Pages 4-5 Sam sets off

Here is Horatio.

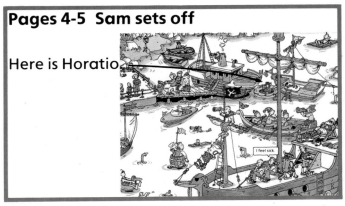

Pages 6-7 Where is Puzzle Island?

Here is the pink elephant.

This is Puzzle Island.

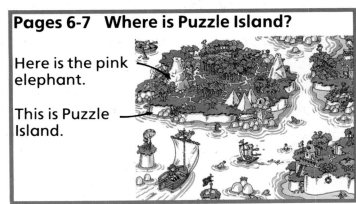

Pages 8-9
The first clue

Here is the red and white stripy arrow.

Pages 10-11
The leafy lake

The way across the lake is marked in red.

Pages 12-13
The safe bridge

This is the safe bridge.

Pages 14-15 Animal spotting

The animals are circled in red.

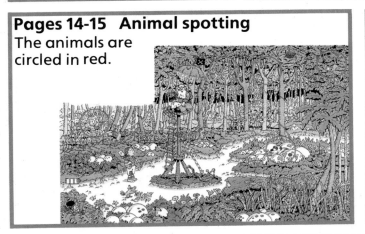

Pages 16-17 The volcano maze

The way to the red flag is marked in red.

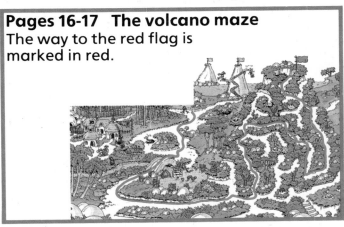

Pages 18-19
Spot the difference

The differences are circled in red.

Pages 20-21
Find the twins

These are the identical twins.

Pages 22-23
Pyramid puzzle
This is the right map. The next clue is in the blue pyramid.

Pages 24-25
Locked out!
Sam can use the key he found on the volcano.

Pages 26-27
The pirate's den
Sam should go through this door.

Pages 28-29 Spies at the waterfall
You don't need an answer to this! Look back through the story and see if you can spot all the characters.

Page 30 The wonderful treasure!
Sam has spotted the skull and crossbones badge. Now he is a real pirate.

Did you spot everything?

Pink Elephants

Pirate Kit

Horatio

The chart below shows you how many pink elephants are hiding on each double page. You can also find out which piece of Sam's pirate kit is hidden on which double page.

Did you remember to look out for Horatio? He may be a sneaky pirate, but he's not as good at hiding as he thinks he is. Look back through the story again and see if you can find him.

Pages	Pink Elephants	Pirate Kit
4-5	Two	Boot
6-7	One	Grog bottle
8-9	Six	Telescope
10-11	Two	Earring
12-13	Two	Spare headscarf
14-15	Three	Hook
16-17	Three	Hornpipe
18-19	One	Compass
20-21	Two	Eyepatch
22-23	Three	Pieces of eight
24-25	Three	Parrot brush
26-27	Two	Cutlass
28-29	Two	Hat
30	Two	

The wonderful treasure
Sam was very happy to find the treasure. He shared it fairly with all his new Puzzle Island friends, but he remembered to save something for his little sister. Even Horatio got a present, and he was so surprised he managed to say thank you!

PUZZLE TOWN

Contents

About this story

There's a fancy dress party in Puzzle Town today. Katy and Tim are invited, but they don't know where to find the party.

An exciting trail of clues and puzzles on every double page will lead them to it. See if you can solve them all and help Katy and Tim on their way. If you get stuck you can look at the answers on pages 63 and 64.

Puzzle Town

Tim

Katy

Fancy dress

Here are Katy's and Tim's fancy dress outfits. One piece is hiding on every double page. If you can't spot them all, the answers on page 64 should help you. Can you guess what Katy and Tim are going as?

Face paints

Joke flower

Big shoes

Hat

Cloak

Funny wig

Spell book

Slippers

Red nose

Striped socks

Wand

Magic kitten

34

Party clues

On some pages there are special party clues, like this one. They will help you find the party, so look out for them.

Party pixie

This is the party pixie. He is in charge of the Puzzle Town party. He helps Katy and Tim on the trail by giving them some important instructions to follow. Keep your eyes peeled.

The party pixie

Odd things

Puzzle Town is a very strange place. If you look very carefully, you will see a lot of odd things. See how many you can spot on every double page.

Boat

Balloon thief

Someone has stolen the Puzzle Town party balloons. The thief is hiding on every double page. Can you spot the balloons he has taken?

Setting off

The day of the Puzzle Town party was sunny and bright. Katy and Tim set off on their trail. In their hands they held a letter from the party pixie.

"First let's work out which Puzzle Town shops we need to go to," said Tim, looking at the letter. "The quicker we do, the quicker we'll find the party."

Which shops must Tim and Katy go to? Can you spot them?

Dear Katy and Tim,
Before you set off on the trail of the Puzzle Town party, here are a few things you must do.
Love from the Party Pixie x x x

Buy some cakes for the party

Get some party hats

Buy party fruit

Collect Katy's new shoes

Post letters

P.S. There are clues along the way and an invitation at the end of the trail. Good luck!

Butcher

Baker's Shop

Lovely cakes

Katy and Tim raced off to the bakers. Here they found some of the most delicious looking cakes they had ever seen. There were gingerbread men and chocolate logs, banana muffins and sugar mice. Katy licked her lips. Which cakes should they take to the party?

   Suddenly Tim spotted a big notice. On it was a special message from the party pixie. It told them exactly which cakes to choose.

Can you find the party cakes?

Best Wheat

Katy and Tim, please bring these cakes to the party.

1 of these

2 of these

3 of these

2 of these

yum yum

Fish cakes

100 cakes

Bumper Book Buns

Cakes'R'Us
Buns for All
Party cakes

38

The toy shop

Next Katy and Tim headed for the toy shop. Here they found Mr Tedd, the owner, puzzling over a chart pinned to the counter.

"The party pixie has told me to wear one of these four costumes to the Puzzle Town party," Mr Tedd explained, pointing to the poster. "I'll work out which one by finding the only toy in my shop that matches one of these pictures. But is it the king, the ghost, the detective or the cowboy?"

Which costume will Mr Tedd wear to the party?

King   Ghost   Detective   Cowboy

41

A fruity puzzle

At the fruit and vegetable shop Katy and Tim looked at all the delicious things and wondered what to choose. Then Katy spotted a blackboard. It was another special message. Katy and Tim read it carefully. Now they knew exactly what fruit to buy. But there was a catch - every fruit had to be different.

What fruit should Tim and Katy choose?

The party is under a big clock.

Oranges

Katy and Tim
Please choose

3 green fruits

4 red fruits

2 yellow fruits

2 orange fruits

Remember - NO two fruits must be the same.

Apple Tree

Doughnut Tree

43

Whose shoes?

With the fruit in their bags, Tim and Katy skipped off to collect Katy's new sandals from the shoe shop. But the shop was in a dreadful mess, and none of the customers had any shoes on at all.

"I'll fetch your sandals in a minute, Katy," said Clive, the assistant. "But first I must find shoes for all these people."

Can you help Clive match the customers with their shoes?

Lots of letters

The Post Office was the last place on their list. Here Katy and Tim found three letter boxes, each for a different type of mail. Zippy mail was for urgent letters, Snail mail was for letters that weren't very important and Air mail was for letters going to another country. Tim and Katy read the Post Office notice board and looked at the stamps on their letters. They soon worked out what they had to do.

Which letters should go into which letter boxes?

Look carefully at your stamps.
Please put all your letters into the right letter boxes.

Zippy mail =
10 Puzzle Pennies

Snail mail =
5 Puzzle Pennies

Air mail =
15 Puzzle Pennies

PARCEL POST

PUD

Nellie

Mrs Ellie Phant. ABROAD

ZIPPY

Tim

Zippy mail only = 10PP

Curious crossings

Now their errands were done, but Tim and Katy still hadn't found the party. Then Tim had a brainwave. They would ask their friend Molly, the mechanic at the Puzzle Town garage, what to do next. She knew everything.

Outside the Post Office, Katy and Tim saw they had to cross lots of roads to reach the garage. They knew the Puzzle Town Road Code - only cross at the striped crossings. But some of the crossings were blocked, so they couldn't cross at these.

Can you find a safe route to the garage using the clear crossings only?

The missing tool kit

At the garage, Katy and Tim found Molly looking for her lost tools. She had lots of Puzzle Town cars to mend.

"I'll help you on your way to the party, if you two help me find my missing tools," said Molly. "I've lost a screwdriver, a saw, a hammer, a torch, a very big nail and my new red cleaning cloth."

Katy and Tim looked around the messy garage. It certainly wasn't going to be an easy job.

Can you find Molly's lost tools?

A puzzling procession

Molly smiled mysteriously. She told the children to follow the group with the most legs in the Puzzle Town procession. There were four groups to choose from - the jolly rollerskaters, the silly skateboards, the prancing ponies and the unusual unicyclists.

Katy and Tim were wondering what she meant, when suddenly they heard laughter and cheering. Racing outside they saw, to their surprise, a strange procession of people and animals. But which was the group with most legs? Then Tim gave a shout. He knew who to follow.

Which group should Tim and Katy follow?

53

The amazing maze

The prancing ponies led Katy and Tim to the Puzzle Town park. When they told the children there was something for them in the middle of the maze, Katy and Tim groaned. The maze was so big and twisty. Would they ever find their way to the middle, and out again?

Can you find the way to the middle of the maze?

54

Map reading

In the middle of the maze, Katy and Tim found an envelope addressed to them. Inside was their party invitation and a message from the party pixie, listing the five clues they had already found. There was also a map, showing the other side of Puzzle Town.

"Now we can find the party," said Katy.

Look at all the clues again. Then look at the map. Where is the party being held?

*Katy and Tim
are invited to the Puzzle Town party
today at 3pm.*

 You will find the party next to three tall trees.

 The party is beside a bridge.

 The party is under a big clock.

 The party is in a street that begins with an 'S'.

 The party is outside a brown building. (It doesn't look like this one).

The above five clues will help you find the Puzzle Town party on the map.

Dear Katy and Tim,
Before you go to the Puzzle Town party, please collect the party guests from Puzzle Town Station.
Love from the Party Pixie ×××

At the station

At last Katy and Tim knew where the party was. But first they had to rush to Puzzle Town station.

"The party guests have arrived," called Joe the guard. "They're waiting for you on the party train."

"Which one is it?" asked Katy.

"It has a green engine, or is it blue? I know it's got spots and is driven by engineer Emma," Joe said.

Can you find the Puzzle Town party train?

58

Puzzle Town Station

59

The Puzzle Town party!

Katy and Tim led the way to the Puzzle Town party, followed by all their new friends. And what a party it was! There were cakes and clowns, jugglers and jellies, bubbles and balloons. Katy and Tim saw lots of familiar faces. Even the mysterious balloon thief was there. As for the party pixie, well he was already planning next year's Puzzle Town party.

How many party guests have you seen before? Can you spot the balloon thief?

Odd things

Did you spot all the odd things going on in Puzzle Town? If not, go back and have another look. If you can't find them, here's a list of all the things Katy and Tim saw on their adventure.

Pages	Odd things
36-37	Sea monster, tiger on a swing, twisty chimney, broken broom handle, duck in boots, the flower shop door is in a strange place!
38-39	Broken chair leg, upside-down teapot spout, a polar bear eating a biscuit, sausages hanging from roof.
40-41	Pickled onions, web-footed doll, aliens, boy with one bare foot.
42-43	Giant legs at crossing, broken trolley handle, duck, tree trunk, doughnut tree.
44-45	Chicks in a box, shoe box full of bananas, child with boot on head, duck in boots.
46-47	Alien photos, parcelled elephant, parcelled snake.
48-49	Ballet-dancing hippo, giraffe in car, monster in pond.
50-51	Dog mechanic, three-wheeled car, snake hose, flowers in exhaust.
52-53	Giraffe in house, feet in roof, dog taking man for a walk.
54-55	Person dressed for winter, upside-down boots, plug in hedge, bird wearing hat, man with three legs.
56-57	Animal with sunglasses, silly street names.
58-59	Tiger dressed as person, lady with upside-down umbrella, strange creatures, ice-skater, firebucket, man in skirt, boat sign.
60-61	What a strange party!

Answers

Pages 36-37
Setting off

These are the shops that Katy and Tim should go to.

Post Office — letters.
Shoe shop — shoes.
Fruit and vegetable shop — fruit.
Bakers — cakes.
Toy shop — party hats.

Pages 38-39
Lovely cakes

The cakes are circled in red.

Pages 40-41 The toy shop

The ghost is the only toy that appears in the shop and on the chart. So Mr Tedd must choose the ghost costume.

Pages 42-43   A fruity puzzle

You could choose several different combinations of fruit. But Katy and Tim chose these:
Green — apple, grape, lime; Red — cherry, plum, strawberry, rhubarb; Yellow — lemon, banana; Orange — peach, orange.

Pages 44-45
Whose shoes?

You can find the shoes and the feet they fit by matching the coloured circles shown here.

Pages 46-47
Lots of letters

Zippy mail
Zippy mail
Snail mail
Snail mail
Air mail
Zippy mail

Pages 48-49   Curious crossings

The route across the clear crossings is marked in red.

Pages 50-51
The missing tools

Molly's missing tools are circled in red.

Pages 52-53
A puzzling procession

The prancing ponies are the group with the most legs in the procession.

Pages 54-55
The amazing maze

The way through the maze is marked in red.

Pages 56-57
Map reading

This is the place where the party is being held. It is the only place on the map that matches all the clues.

Pages 58-59
At the station

This is the Puzzle Town party train.

Pages 60-61
The Puzzle Town party!

This is the balloon thief.

Look back through the story and see if you can spot all the people who are now at the party.

Did you spot everything?
Fancy dress

The chart below shows you which piece of either Katy's or Tim's fancy dress costume is hidden on which double page. Katy's costume is a wizard, and Tim's is a clown.

Pages	Fancy dress
36-37	Magic kitten
38-39	Spell book
40-41	Joke flower
42-43	Wand
44-45	Striped socks
46-47	Slippers
48-49	Red nose
50-51	Cloak
52-53	Big shoes
54-55	Hat
56-57	Face paints
58-59	Funny wig

Balloon thief

Did you remember to look out for that naughty balloon thief? At least he brought the balloons to the party in the end!

Next year's party . . .

The party pixie is already looking forward to next year's Puzzle Town party. He is planning all sorts of puzzles and wonderful surprises. Katy and Tim are very excited about the plans for next year's party too, but they have a special request. Next year, they'd like to get their invitation through the mail, like everyone else.

PUZZLE FARM

Contents

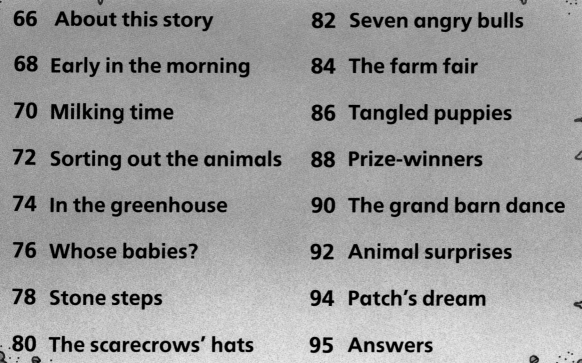

About this story

This story is about Beth and Harry and their adventures on Puzzle Farm.

Puzzle Farm

Beth   Harry

We will be back in time for the fair!

Tilly, the Puzzle Farmer, and all her farm helpers have gone on a day trip to Puzzle Island. Beth and Harry are in charge of Puzzle Farm for the day. They have a lot to do as it's the farm fair in the afternoon. Some of their friends from nearby Puzzle Town have come to help them out.

armhands   Tilly

Puzzle Town friends

You will find a puzzle on every double page. See if you can solve them all and help Beth, Harry and the Puzzle Town people get everything ready for the fair. If you get stuck, you can look at the answers on pages 95 and 96.

The musical instruments

Tilly and her helpers have planned a surprise for after the fair. For this they will need their musical instruments. One instrument is hidden on almost every double page. Here you can see them all.

cymbals
fiddle

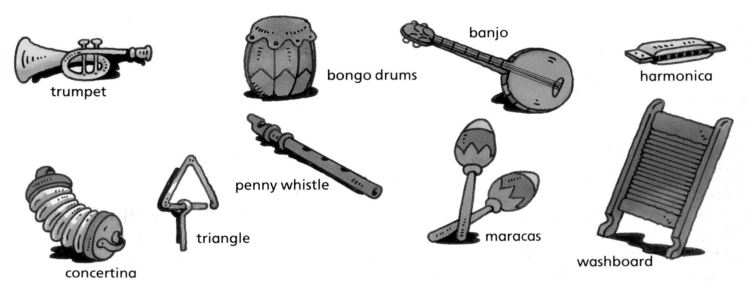
trumpet
bongo drums
banjo
harmonica
penny whistle
triangle
maracas
washboard
concertina

Patch
Patch is the farm puppy. Beth and Harry want to enter him in the puppy competition. But Patch has other ideas. He is hiding on every double page.

Can you spot him?

Purple puzzle mice
Puzzle Farm is the home of the only purple puzzle mice in the world. There is at least one mouse hiding on every double page. Keep your eyes open!

Early in the morning

On the day of the fair, Harry and Beth woke up early. There was a lot to do on Puzzle Farm.

First they had to feed the pony, the pig, the chicken, the duck and the rabbit. These were the animals that lived in the farmyard. But there was no sign of them. And where was Patch, the naughty farm puppy? Beth and Harry had to keep a special eye out for him.

Can you find all the farmyard animals?

Milking time

Beth and Harry fed the farmyard animals and then followed Patch's pawprints to the milking shed. Here they found Clive from Puzzle Town.

"I have to milk these cows," he wailed. "But I can't put them in the right milking stalls because I don't know their names."

"That's easy," said Beth. "Each cow looks like her name."

Can you see where each cow should go?

HATTY

16 SPOT

BIG SPOTS   SHAGGY   BELLE   SOCKS

Sorting out the animals

Outside the milking shed, Harry and Beth heard noises coming from the next field. They raced over and saw Mr Stamp the postman. He was looking at lots of different animals.

"Tilly told me to divide these animals into three groups ready for the fair," he said. "There's the spotty group, the feathered creatures and the animals with horns. But I can't work out which animals belong in which group."

Can you?

We don't belong in any of the groups.

73

In the greenhouse

Their next stop was the greenhouse. Tilly had given Harry and Beth special instructions to pick five flowers for the farm fair. She didn't mind what they looked like, as long as every flower was a different kind and a different colour.

Can you find five different flowers?

Whose babies?

In the field behind the greenhouse, Harry and Beth saw all kinds of animals wandering about. In the middle of them stood Mrs Bagel, the baker, scratching her head.

"These mother animals have lost their babies," she said. "I know the babies look just like their mothers, but I still can't match them up."

Can you match the baby animals with their mothers?

Stone steps

Their tasks were nearly finished when Beth remembered Tilly's best hat. It had been lent to one of the scarecrows and Harry and Beth had to find it in time for the fair.

The scarecrows were in a far away field surrounded by high walls. The only way through was the stone steps. But some of the steps weren't safe to climb and some were blocked.

Can you find a way across the fields to the scarecrows?

The scarecrows' hats

Beth and Harry arrived, puffing and panting at the field of scarecrows. There was a surprise waiting for them. All the scarecrows were wearing hats! Which one was Tilly's? Then Harry remembered that Tilly's hat was mostly red, and the flowers on it weren't blue or green. It should be easy to find.

Which is Tilly's hat?

Seven angry bulls

In the next field, Mr Tedd the toy shop man, was struggling to control seven angry bulls.

"I must keep these bullies apart," he cried. "But they all have to stay in this field. I've got these three special anti-bull poles to separate them. I've put one pole down, and now I don't know where the other two should go.

Can you fit the other two poles so that each bull is in a separate part of the field?

The farm fair

At last Beth and Harry finished all their tasks. Excitedly they set off for the fair. At the entrance they found Joe, the station master, looking very worried.

"The fair is about to start," he said. "My job was to meet Tilly. She's opening the fair. But she's not here and we can't start without her."

Can you see Tilly at the fair?

PONY RACE

FATTEST HEN CONTEST

Lost PETS

Smelliest Flower Contest

Prettiest Piggy

FRUIT STALL

WELCOME TO THE PUZZLE FARM FAIR

LOG SAWING

85

Tangled puppies

Beth and Harry breathed a sigh of relief. The fair had begun! Then they remembered the puppy competition. They raced to the main show ring, but Patch was nowhere to be seen. Inside the ring, the competition had begun. It was very confusing. Each contestant had two puppies, but the leads were all tangled up, and no one knew whose puppies were whose.

Can you untangle the leads and find out which puppies belong to which child?

Prize-winners

At five o'clock everyone went to the judges' tent for the prize giving ceremony. But the prize-winners' list was lost. Now no one knew who should win which prize, or what competition they had entered. Beth and Harry looked at the prize-winners – the horse, the hen, the flowers, the cake and the pig. Then they thought back to all they had seen at the fair that day. Soon they knew which prize each had won.

Can you match the prizes to the winners?

The grand barn dance

But the fun wasn't over yet. That night, to celebrate the fair, there was a grand barn dance at Puzzle Farm. All the farm hands were back from their holiday. They played their instruments loudly as everyone danced the farmyard fling. But Mabel and Doris Green from the fruit and vegetable shop weren't smiling. They needed six red apples to finish making the fizzy farmyard fruit punch, and they couldn't see them anywhere.

Can you find the six red apples?

Animal surprises

When the music stopped, Harry and Beth heard another sound in the distance. They tiptoed quietly out into the dark night. The noise was getting louder and it came from the animal shed. Creeping nearer, they peered in through the window and saw a strange sight. The animals were having their very own barn dance! And at last Beth and Harry had found Patch.

How many animals have you seen before?
Where is Patch?

93

finding the babies

looking over the stone step

in the scarecrow field

near the greenhouse

near the bulls

Patch's dream

After the barn dance, Patch fell asleep and dreamed of the things he had done earlier that day. Look carefully at Patch's dream pictures and you will discover the story of the naughty puppy's day. If you didn't spot him on every page, these pictures should help you to find him.

outside the milking shed

at the farm fair

LUCKY DIP

escaping the puppy competition

ATCHOO

at milking time

in the farmyard

at the prize giving

Answers

Pages 68-69   Early in the morning
The farmyard animals are circled in red.

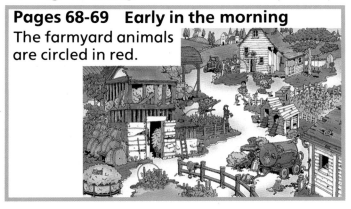

Pages 70-71   Milking time

Shaggy · 16 spots · Socks · Big spots · Hatty · Belle

Pages 72-73   Sorting out the animals

feathers spots horns   horns   spots

feathers

Pages 74-75
In the greenhouse
You could choose several different combinations of flowers, but Beth and Harry chose these:

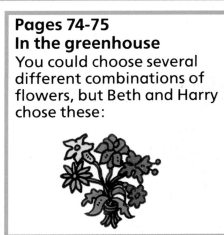

Pages 76-77   Whose babies?

E   A   b   D   B   f   a   C

g

c

d

h   G   F   H   e

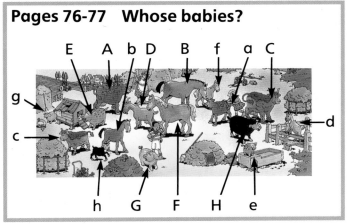

Pages 78-79   Stone steps
The way over the stone steps is marked in red.

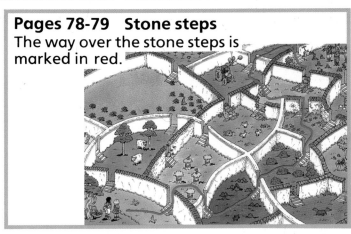

Pages 80-81
The scarecrows' hats
This is Tilly's hat.

Pages 82-83   Seven angry bulls
The two missing poles are shown in red.

Pages 84-85　The farm fair

Tilly is here.

Pages 86-87　Tangled puppies

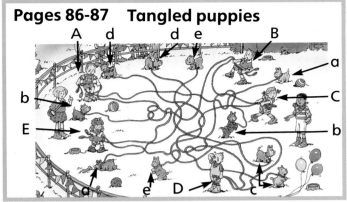

Pages 88-89
Prize-winners

Prize	Winner
Cup	Flowers
Shield	Cake
Blue rosette	Pony
Red rosette	Hen
Green rosette	Pig

Pages 90-91　The grand barn dance
The six red apples are circled in black.

Pages 92-93
Animal surprises

Patch is here.

Look back through the book and see if you can spot all the animals who are now at the animal barn dance.

Did you spot everything?

Purple puzzle mice

Musical instruments

Pages	Purple puzzle mice	Musical instrument
68-69	five	banjo
70-71	three	triangle
72-73	five	cymbals
74-75	four	penny whistle
76-77	five	washboard
78-79	two	maracas
80-81	four	concertina
82-83	five	harmonica
84-85	three	trumpet
86-87	two	bongo drum
88-89	three	fiddle
90-91	three	
92-93	three	

PUZZLE CASTLE

Contents

About this story

This story is about a brave knight called Sophie and her adventure at Puzzle Castle. There is a puzzle on every double page. Solve them all and help Sophie on her way. If you get stuck, look at the answers on pages 127 and 128.

This is Sophie, the brave knight. She lives in a village not far from Puzzle Castle.

This is Puzzle Castle.

Sophie's friend, Titus the Timid, lives in Puzzle Castle. He has written Sophie a letter. Here it is.

This is Titus. He is wearing his banquet outfit.

Puzzle Castle
Monday

Dear Sophie,

You are invited to a grand banquet in Puzzle Castle today, but first we need your help. For the past three days there has been a monster in the dungeons. No one has seen it, but everyone is very scared. You are the bravest person I know. Could you come early and get rid of it? I will meet you in the castle courtyard at three o'clock.

Love from your friend, Titus.

P.S. I will be wearing my new banquet outfit!

98

Useful equipment

When Sophie gets to the castle she will need to find ten things that may come in handy when she reaches the dungeons. You will find one object on every double page, from the moment she enters the castle, until she arrives at the monster's lair...

umbrella

powerful flashlight

monster protection shield

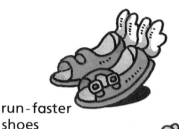
run-faster shoes

monster phrase book

monster protection helmet

key

mystery box

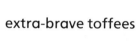
extra-brave toffees

useful string

Cecil the castle ghost

Puzzle Castle is haunted by a very friendly ghost. His name is Cecil. He is hiding spookily on every double page. See if you can spot him.

Jester Jim

Jester Jim is practising his juggling for the banquet, but he's not very good at it. He has lost his juggling balls around the castle. There is at least one hiding on every double page. Can you find them?

The juggling balls look like this.

The adventure starts

On the day of the grand banquet, Sophie set out for Puzzle Castle. As she drew near, the castle loomed ahead of her, surrounded by a monstrous moat. Peering down into the water she saw strange creatures and big fish with snappy teeth.

The only way across the water was by the many bridges. But this wasn't as easy as it looked. Some of the bridges were broken and others were too dangerous to cross. Sophie would have to be very careful.

Can you find a safe route across the moat?

Where is Titus?

Sophie jumped to the safety of the bank. She bounded up to the castle gate and pulled the bell which jangled loudly. The gate rose slowly and Sophie stepped into the bustling courtyard of Puzzle Castle.

Everyone was busy preparing for the grand banquet and trying hard not to think about the monster in the dungeons. It was nearly three o' clock. Sophie looked out for Titus. She was sure he was hiding somewhere.

Can you see Titus?

grrrr!

boo!

Sophie's instructions

"Don't worry, Titus, I'll deal with the monster," said Sophie bravely. "Lead me to the dungeons."

"Oh no, Sophie," Titus shivered. "You are brave enough to find the monster by yourself. Here's a plan of Puzzle Castle, and a list of people you will meet on your journey. You must visit each person in turn. Each one needs your help getting ready for the banquet. Help them out and you will soon find your way to the dungeons."

Can you match the people with the rooms where Sophie is most likely to find them?

FIND THESE PEOPLE ON THE WAY

MERVIN, Portrait Keeper

PRINCESS POSY

LARRY, Look-out boy

BETH the Babysitter

MRS. CRUMB the Cook

WIZARD WILF

104

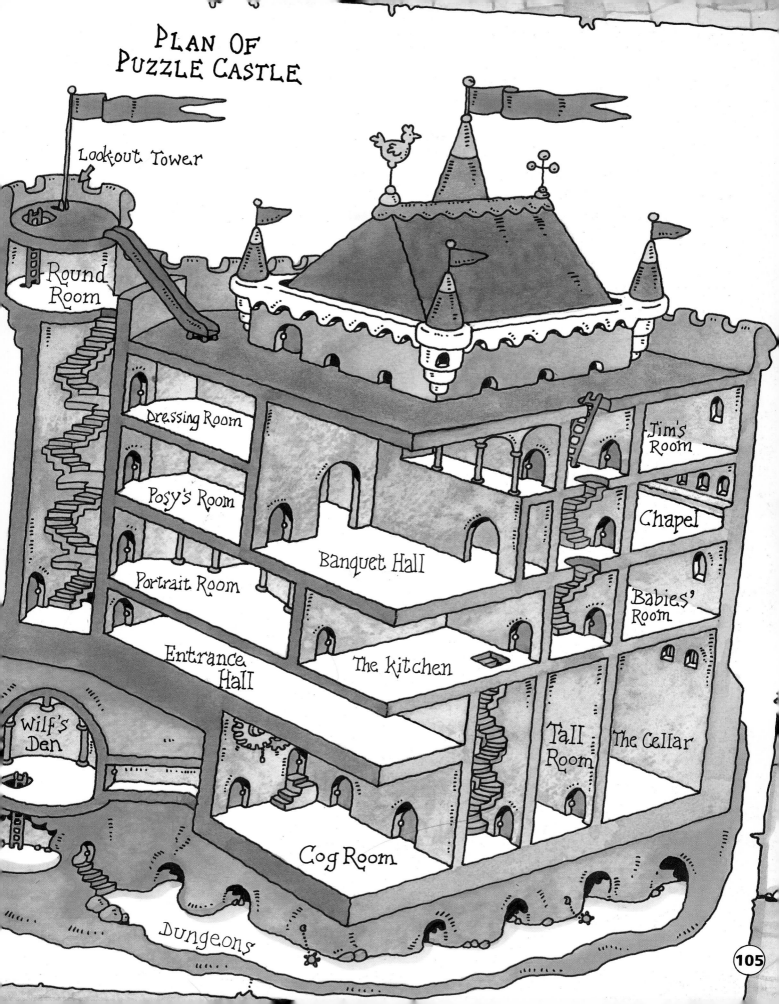

PLAN OF PUZZLE CASTLE

Lookout Tower

Round Room

Dressing Room

Posy's Room

Portrait Room

Entrance Hall

Wilf's Den

Banquet Hall

The Kitchen

Cog Room

Jim's Room

Chapel

Babies' Room

Tall Room

The Cellar

Dungeons

Royal portraits

Sophie promised to see Titus later and began her journey. Her first stop was the portrait gallery.

"Sophie," cried Mervin the portrait keeper. "Princess Posy's Uncle Edwin is coming all the way from Gruldavia for the banquet. I have to meet him, but I've forgotten what he looks like. If I get this wrong, I'll be thrown in the dungeons. His picture is here. He has black hair, a beard and a moustache. He always wears red and purple. He has no children and he doesn't like horses."

Can you find Uncle Edwin's picture?

Does Uncle Edwin have big ears?

Princess Posy's problem

Sophie curtsied as she entered Princess Posy's room. What a mess it was!

"Sophie!" cried Posy. "I know you're going to fight the monster, but I've got a bigger problem. I want to wear my matching necklace, bracelet, ring and crown to the banquet. I can't find them in my big wooden chest."

Can you find a necklace, a bracelet, a ring and a crown that match?

The look-out tower

Sophie left Posy admiring her jewels, and climbed up to the castle battlements. Here she found Larry the look-out boy, pointing to a lot of people approaching the castle.

"Sophie!" he cried. "All these people are arriving for the grand banquet, but I don't know if they've been invited."

Banquet guest list

BARON BORIS the BAD and his BADDIES (not invited - deserves 3 bad eggs)

SIR HORACE and his HORRIBLES (not invited - deserves soup treatment)

SIR NICE NED and his FRIENDS (invited)

COUNT CURTIS and his CRAFTY COUSINS (not invited - bubbling treacle treatment)

LADY LUCY LOVELY and FRIENDS (invited)

FEARLESS FREDA and FRIENDS (invited)

WONDERFUL WANDA and her FRIENDS (invited)

NASTY KNIGHT KEVIN and NASTIES (not invited - aim rubber arrows at him)

BAD EGGS

DUNG

SOUP

BUBBLING TREACLE

Sophie read the guest list. Then she looked at the flags of the approaching groups and checked to see if they were invited or not.

Do you know who is invited to the banquet?

Beth and the babies

Sophie scrambled down to the babies' room. Here she found Beth, the very new babysitter, and lots of naughty babies.

"Sophie," cried Beth. "I have to dress the babies for the banquet, but I don't know which clothes belong to which baby. I've even forgotten each baby's name!"

Sophie looked at the party outfits hanging on the wall. Then she looked at the babies in their underwear. Soon she had matched them together.

Can you find the right outfit for each baby?

113

In the kitchen

Sophie left Beth with the smartly dressed babies and followed the smell of burnt banquet buns to the kitchen. The grand banquet feast was boiling away, but Mrs. Crumb the cook was flustered.

"I wanted to make you a monster-fighting pudding to build up your strength, Sophie," she said. "But some rascal has hidden the ingredients. I've lost two red plums, a pot of honey, three fresh eggs, four loaves of bread and a lemon."

Can you find the missing pudding ingredients?

COOKIES

biscuits

Mustard

Which way now?

"I'll have to eat that pudding later!" Sophie called, as she dropped through the trapdoor. She climbed down some steep steps. To the right was a door. She pushed it open and walked into a room with cogs hanging from the ceiling. There was no one here, so Sophie decided to move on.

Her next stop was Wizard Wilf's den. But which door led to it? There were six to choose from, but danger lurked behind almost every one. Sophie looked at her castle plan and soon knew which door to take.

Which door should Sophie choose?

The wizard's den

Wizard Wilf's Den
it's secret

Sophie pushed open the door and walked down a small passageway to another door. Through this door lay Wizard Wilf's secret den. Wilf stood stirring a big pot.

"Sophie," he cried. "I'm brewing a magic potion to cast a spell. It will make you invisible and help you dodge the monster."

Before...

Sophie held her breath as Wilf waved his magic wand. There was a purple flash and a puff of smoke, but when it had cleared they saw the spell hadn't quite worked. Sophie was still there, but lots of other things had vanished.

How many things have disappeared?
Can you spot them all?

After...

Sophie finds the way

There was no time to waste. Sophie climbed down Wilf's ladder and crept along an underground passageway. She soon found herself at the beginning of a maze of tunnels. In the distance she could hear the terrible roars of the monster. She didn't want to get lost underground as she made her way towards the roars, so she unravelled her ball of useful string as she went.

Can you find the way to the monster's roars?

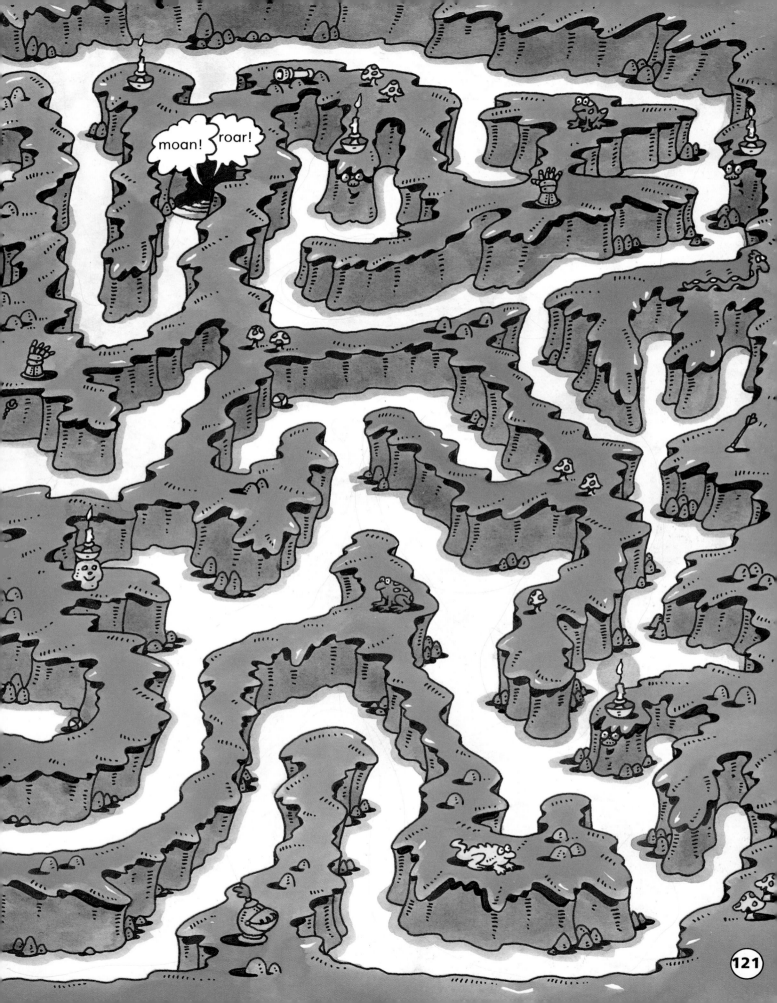

The monster's lair...

The rumbling and roaring noise grew louder as Sophie reached the end of the maze. She was at the top of a small flight of steps.

Sophie checked she had all her equipment with her. Chewing nervously on an extra-brave toffee, Sophie began her final journey, down the winding staircase to the monster's lair. . .

She checked her monster phrase book.

She turned the key.

Hello. Are you a friendly monster?

Og gob glook?

Where's the station?

Zip zap zop?

She opened the door and saw...

...a little dragon, crying and sniffing. Was this the fierce monster of Puzzle Castle? Could Sophie cheer him up?

Hello ... hic ... sob. My name's Dennis. I got stuck in this scary dungeon. I'm hungry and cold and I've lost my mum.

Then she remembered. She could give him the one piece of equipment she hadn't used yet.

What can Sophie give Dennis?

The grand banquet

Dennis cheered up at once. Then Sophie had another idea. She would take him to the banquet. Sophie led Dennis back through the castle and up to the grand banquet hall.

At first everyone was scared of Dennis. But they soon saw he wasn't a monster at all. He was a very friendly little dragon who liked to dance. Everyone was very pleased to see him.

There is someone in this picture who is especially happy to see Dennis. Do you know who it is?

124

Bedtime story

After the banquet, everyone was very tired. Just before bedtime, Sophie, Titus and Posy curled up with their cups of castle cocoa and listened as Dennis told the story of his adventure at Puzzle Castle . . .

Boris's army pounded past. The ground shook.

Heavy earth fell in front of the tunnel. I was trapped inside.

I saw a tunnel in the hill and I hid inside.

I could only go on, deeper into the tunnel, until I reached the castle dungeon.

Suddenly I saw Boris the Bad and his baddies coming my way. I was very scared.

I was there for three days, getting hungrier and hungrier, until Sophie rescued me.

On Saturday I was playing on the hill beside Puzzle Castle.

I'll never forget the friends I made today.

Answers

Pages 100-101 The adventure starts

The route to the castle is shown in red.

Pages 102-103 Where is Titus?

Titus is here.

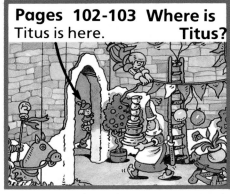

Pages 104-105 Sophie's instructions

Person	Room
Mervin	Portrait Room
Princess Posy	Posy's Room
Larry	Look-out Tower
Beth	Babies' Room
Mrs. Crumb	Kitchen
Wizard Wilf	Wilf's Den

Pages 106-107 Royal portraits

This is Uncle Edwin.

Pages 108-109 Princess Posy's problem

Posy's matching jewels are circled in red.

Pages 110-111 The look-out tower

Lady Lucy Lovely, Sir Nice Ned and Fearless Freda are all invited to the banquet. Baron Boris the Bad and his baddies aren't invited.

Pages 112-113 Beth and the babies

Joe
Jack
George
Amber
Frank
Kezi
Freya

Now you know each baby's name, you can match them with their outfits.

Pages 114-115 In the kitchen

The missing ingredients are circled in red.

Pages 116-117 Which way now?

Sophie should go through this door.

Pages 118-119
The wizard's den
The red circles show where Wilf's things were.

Pages 120-121
Sophie finds the way
The way to the monster is shown in red.

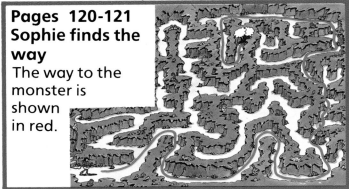

Pages 122-123 The monster's lair...
Sophie gives Dennis the mystery box she found in the wizard's den. It is a dragon-in-a-box!

Pages 124-125 The grand banquet
Dennis's mum is especially happy to see him. Here she is.

Did you spot everything?

Juggling balls

Useful equipment

Cecil the ghost

The chart below shows you how many juggling balls are hidden on each double page. You can also find out which piece of Sophie's useful equipment is hidden where.

Did you remember to look out for Cecil the ghost? He is hiding spookily on every double page. Look back through the book again and see if you can find him.

Pages	Juggling balls	Useful equipment
100-101	one	none here!
102-103	four	monster protection shield
104-105	one	key
106-107	three	useful string
108-109	four	run-faster shoes
110-111	two	umbrella
112-113	three	monster phrase book
114-115	five	extra-brave toffees
116-117	two	monster protection helmet
118-119	three (or is it six?)	mystery box
120-121	four	powerful flashlight
122-123	one	none here!
124-125	nineteen	none here!

Four friends
Now Sophie, Titus, Dennis and Princess Posy are very good friends. Every Saturday when the sun is shining, they play on the hill beside Puzzle Castle. If it's raining, they eat toast and cakes in Posy's room, and Jester Jim teaches them how to juggle. And because he has three new friends to play with, Dennis isn't afraid of Boris the Bad anymore.

PUZZLE PLANET

Contents

About this story

This story is about a young astronaut called Archie, his robot Blip, and their adventures on Puzzle Planet. There is a puzzle on every double page. See if you can solve them all. If you get stuck, you can look at the answers on pages 159 and 160.

Archie

Blip

Archie's space base

Space school report

NAME: Archie

SUBJECT	GRADE
STAR SPOTTING	A+
ROCKET FLYING	A+
MOON WALKING	A+

Comment:
Archie is a very helpful member of class.

Archie's school report

Archie is a junior astronaut who goes to space school. One day, in the summer, he gets a surprise letter. It is from the wisest astronaut teacher of them all, Professor Moon. Here is the letter.

Golden Palace
Puzzle Planet
Wednesday

To: Archie
    Space base
    Planet Earthy Minor

Dear Archie,
        I have read your space school report. Well done! Now you and some of your school friends have the chance to prove your skills as astronauts. You must travel to Puzzle Planet and find me in my Golden Palace by 4 o'clock on Thursday. If you succeed, I will award you with a special space badge which I only give to the bravest young astronauts in the universe.

        From Professor Moon.

        P.S. I will send you a kit list of the things you need to bring to Puzzle Planet

Puzzle Planet

Professor Moon

Things to spot

All good astronauts are observant. As soon as Archie arrives on Puzzle Planet, he must prove he is a good astronaut by spotting some special objects. These objects can only be found on Puzzle Planet. There is one hiding on each double page, from the moment Archie lands. Here they are.

giant pink marshmallow

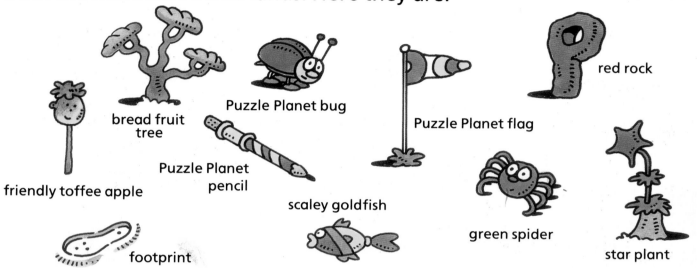

friendly toffee apple

bread fruit tree

Puzzle Planet bug

Puzzle Planet pencil

scaley goldfish

Puzzle Planet flag

red rock

green spider

star plant

footprint

Sneaky Sydney

Sydney lives on Puzzle Planet. He's a bit of a bully and likes spoiling people's games. Look out for Sydney's spy satellite. It's watching Archie on every double page.

Sydney's spy satellite.

Sydney

Space school report
NAME: Sydney

SUBJECT	GRADE
COMET CRUISING PLANET HOPPING	E -
BEING FRIENDLY	E -

comment:
Sydney could try harder.
He is rather disruptive.

Space newts

Puzzle Planet is the home of the pink space newts. There is at least one newt hiding on every double page, from the time Archie lands on Puzzle Planet. Look out for them!

Now turn the page to begin the adventure !

Getting ready

Archie was looking forward to his very first visit to Puzzle Planet. Outside, his rocket was parked and was nearly ready for take off.

Archie looked at the kit list Professor Moon had sent him. It showed six useful things he would need to take to Puzzle Planet. Archie looked around his small space base in dismay. It was such a mess, how would he ever find the six things on the list?

Can you find the six things Archie needs?

KIT-LIST. Bring these things with you to Puzzle Planet. From Professor Moon.

tracker beam - for contacting other astronauts when in trouble (makes a beeping noise)

Puzzle Planet guide book

one space-buggy (exactly like this one)

one cosmic compass (exactly like this one)

bionic binoculars (exactly like these)

list of school friends going to Puzzle Planet to collect their special space badges

Star maze

Soon everything was ready for the journey. Now Archie had to plan his route to Puzzle Planet. He peered through his super-powerful telescope. Far, far away, he could see the red glow of Puzzle Planet.

In his little space base, Archie shivered and wondered if he would ever find a path through the twisty maze of stars shining in the galaxy.

Can you help Archie find a way through the star maze to Puzzle Planet?

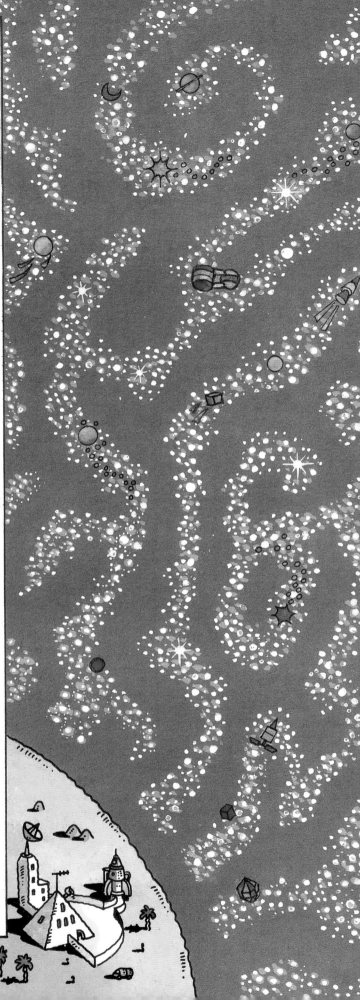

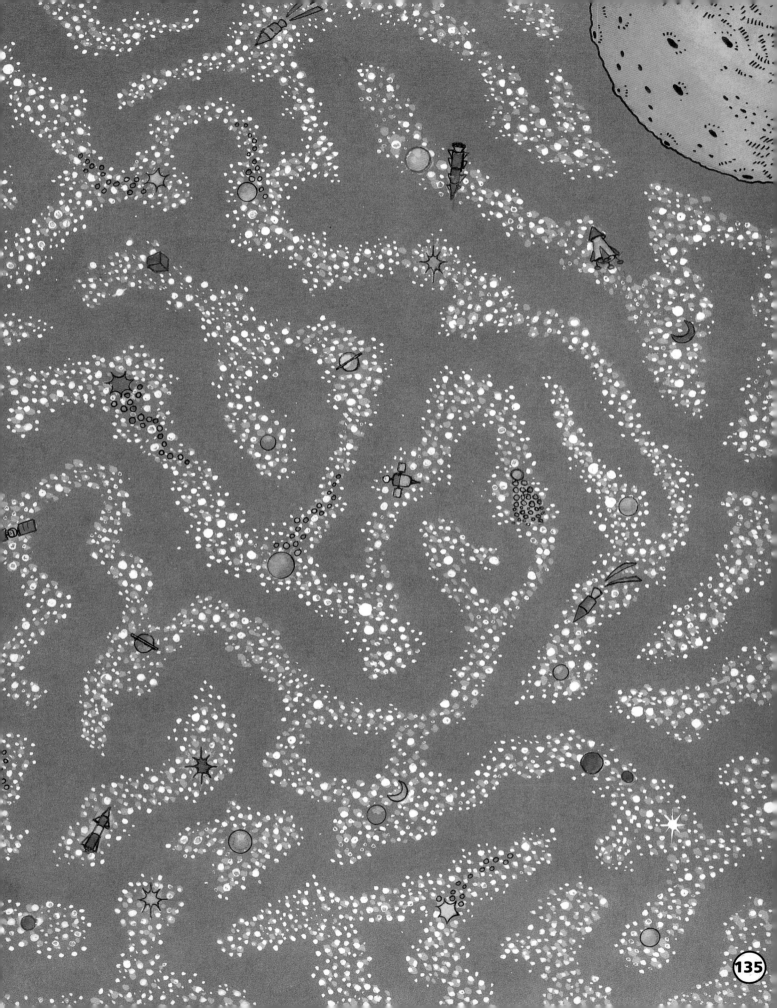

Space journey

At last it was time to set off. Archie made some final flight checks, took his travel-sickness pill and called to Blip. The two friends climbed aboard the space rocket. They closed the outer doors, fastened their seat belts and set the controls for Puzzle Planet.

Archie began the countdown. "5...4...3...2...1..."

They sped through stars...

...and cruised on past comets.

They were nearly there when...

...The rocket dived out of control. They were going to crash on Puzzle Planet!

Planet puzzle

Archie was very pleased to see Blip again. Now they had to find out exactly where they were on Puzzle Planet.

Archie spun his cosmic compass and walked a little way north into a small clearing. There were lots of strange things to look at. Archie got out his Puzzle Planet guide book and turned to the page he needed. He looked at the pictures carefully. By matching the pictures with what he saw in front of him, he could find out where they were.

Where are they?

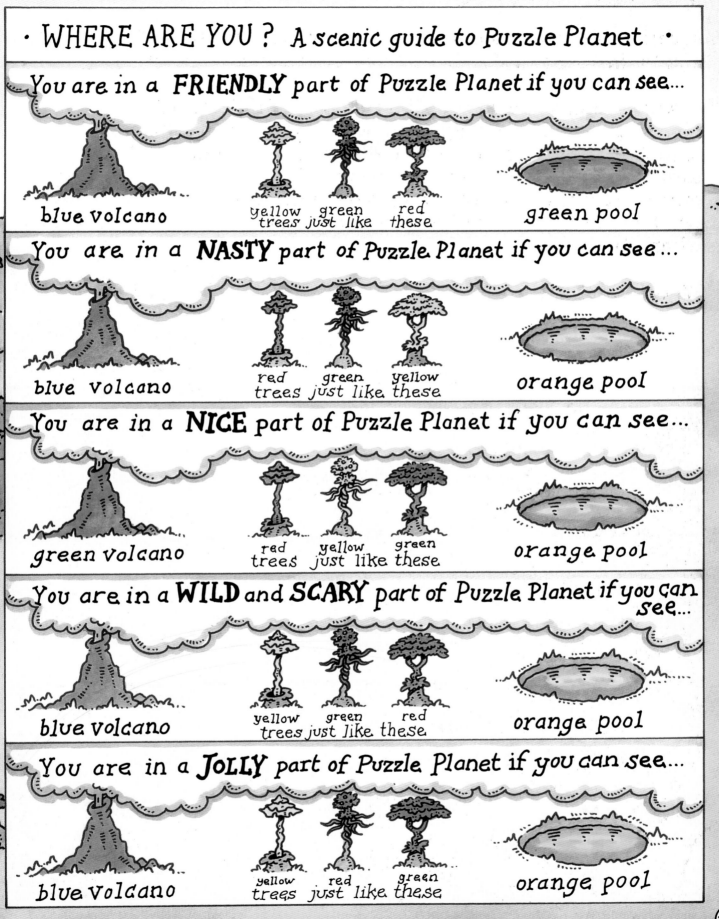

· WHERE ARE YOU ? A scenic guide to Puzzle Planet ·

You are in a **FRIENDLY** part of Puzzle Planet if you can see...

blue volcano   yellow green red trees just like these   green pool

You are in a **NASTY** part of Puzzle Planet if you can see...

blue volcano   red green yellow trees just like these   orange pool

You are in a **NICE** part of Puzzle Planet if you can see...

green volcano   red yellow green trees just like these   orange pool

You are in a **WILD** and **SCARY** part of Puzzle Planet if you can see...

blue volcano   yellow green red trees just like these   orange pool

You are in a **JOLLY** part of Puzzle Planet if you can see...

blue volcano   yellow red green trees just like these   orange pool

Archie in trouble

Archie gulped. They were in a wild and scary part of Puzzle Planet! Suddenly there was a buzzing noise behind them. Archie spun around. It came from the rocket wreck. Archie and Blip rushed over to investigate. The video screen was on and someone was sending a message. It was Sydney, the space school bully.

"Archie, my magnetic field made you crash. I have done the same to three of your two-eyed, two-eared space mates. You won't get your special badges from Professor Moon now. Tee hee."

The picture faded. Archie picked up the list of his school friends who were also on their way to Professor Moon's palace. Archie thought back to Sydney's words, and soon knew which three friends were in trouble, somewhere on Puzzle Planet.

Which of Archie's space friends are in trouble?

Jane from Jupiter	Martin the Martian	Bob from Beta Milennia
Cosmic Ray	Nellie from Neptune	Asteroid Annie
Betty from Blarg	Ollie from Outer Space	Astro Phil
Spacey Sall	Sadie from Saturn	Victor the Vargon
Galactic Greg	Supernova Sam	Pluto Poppy
Milky-way Mary	Pete from Planet Putty	Archie from Earthy Minor

Ice storm

There was no time to lose. Archie had to find his friends. He switched on his tracker beam. If another astronaut was in trouble he'd soon find out. Sure enough, it began to beep. Archie pulled the space-buggy from the wreckage, put it into mega-drive, and zoomed off.

Within seconds they were speeding past strange snowy scenery. Suddenly a huge ball of ice fell from the sky.

"It's an ice-meteor storm!" Archie cried. "We must find shelter before it smashes us into pieces!"

Can you see a safe, empty cave where Archie, Blip and the buggy can find shelter?

Bubble trouble

The storm passed and they drove safely on. Ahead, on top of a small mountain, a rocket had crashed. Someone was in trouble! All of a sudden a big bubble floated past. Trapped inside was Pete from Planet Putty. Archie was about to burst the bubble when he saw another one, with another Pete inside, then another, and another.

"I bet this is Sydney's trick," thought Archie. "Only one is the real Pete. The rest are slightly different."

Which is the real Pete?

Spacey swamp

Pete jumped aboard the buggy and they bounced on. Soon they came to a stop at a slimy green swamp. In the middle was Betty from Blarg, trapped on top of her sinking rocket. They had to rescue her and reach the other side to continue their journey.

Pete was an expert on swamps. He knew that there was only one safe way to cross. They must step from one plant or creeper to the next. But they musn't tread on anything with red spots. They would have to be very careful.

Can you rescue Betty and reach the other side?

Giant snails

Back on dry land, the friends saw a space ship surrounded by giant snails. Inside was a worried Victor the Vargon.

"These slimy creatures are hungry!" he cried.

"It's OK, Victor," yelled Betty. "The Puzzle Planet snails like eating blue space bananas best, and I can see seven, one for each of them!"

Can you find seven blue bananas?

148

149

Following the signal

"Now let's find Professor Moon," said Archie, as the snails began to eat the blue bananas.

They were just wondering which way to go when Archie's tracker beam began to beep. Someone else was in trouble. The noise came from the end of the path ahead.

They ran up the path to a funny shaped building.

The door was open, so they walked slowly inside . . .

The beep got louder.

They followed the noise along a winding passage.

150

At the end was a small room, but there was no one in trouble here. Then Archie knew they had been tricked. There were things in this room he had seen before.

What things has Archie seen before?
Who do you think they belong to?

Trapped!

They were in Sydney's secret hide-out. In the room ahead stood Sydney himself.

"You walked straight into my trap," he smiled. "There's no escape. You won't find Professor Moon now."

Everyone was very scared, but Blip wasn't afraid. He looked at Sydney and his antenna began to twitch. He knew exactly how to make Sydney disappear and give the space friends time to escape.

What can the friends do to make Sydney disappear?

SYDNEY'S BEST TRICKS TO PLAY ON FRIENDS

BLACK HOLE – *friend sits in dark for ten mega-minutes*

GARBAGE CHUTE – *covers friend in galactic garbage*

TRAP NET – *friend caught inside for six mega-minutes*

TELEPORTER – *sends friend to an unknown destination for one mega-hour*

152

Canyon maze

Blip flicked the teleporter switch on and Sydney vanished. The friends dived through the door on the other side of the room, pausing to grab some useful skateboards. They skated down a chute and skidded to a stop at the edge of a maze of canyons. In the distance they could see three gold buildings.

"One of those is Professor Moon's palace!" cried Betty. "I recognize it from his letter. We'll skate there in no time."

Which is Professor Moon's palace?
Can you find a way to it?

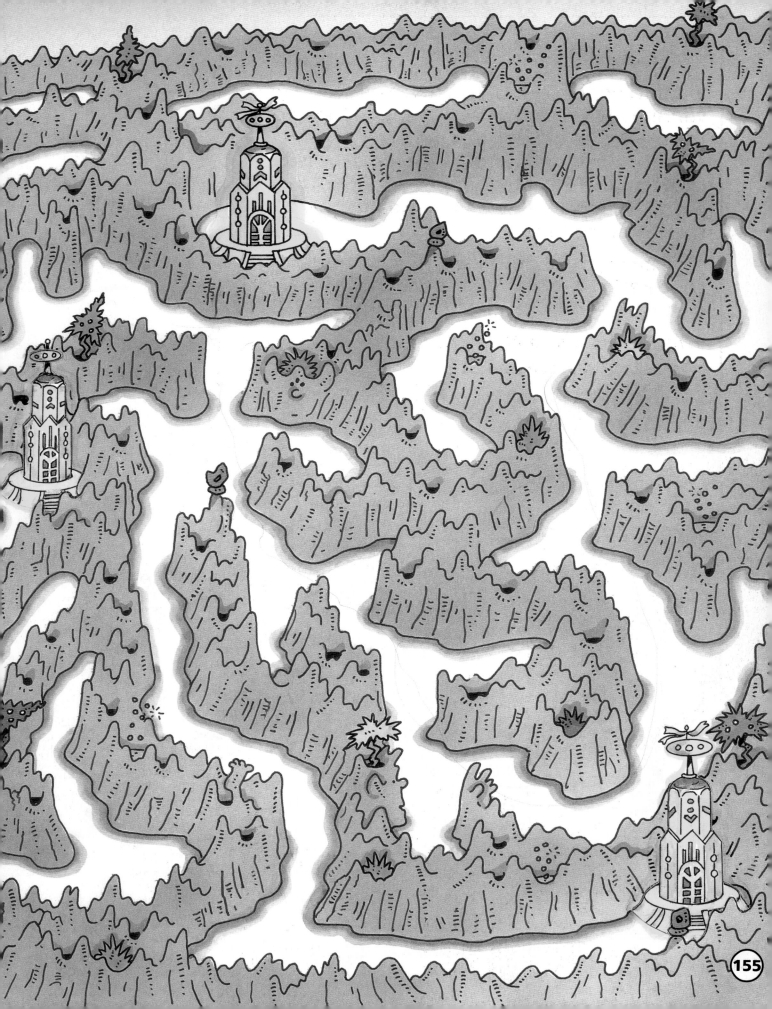

Just in time

Archie and his friends skated into the palace, just as the clock struck four. They saw lots of familiar faces, all smiling and cheering.

"If it wasn't for Archie, we wouldn't have made it to the palace at all," said Betty.

She told everyone about their adventures. Professor Moon gave Archie an extra award for being especially brave. Even Blip had a tasty treat. They were very proud and pleased.

**Do you recognize everyone here?
Can you spot the unexpected guest?**

Spacey Shortbread

Volcano Cake

Planet Pudding

Puzzle Pop

Puzzle Planet creatures

Did you notice that there are some very strange creatures living on Puzzle Planet? Below is a page from Archie's guide book. It shows pictures of some of them.

You can also read about each creature. Whereabouts on Puzzle Planet do you think each one lives? Why not see if you can find them all?

YOU MIGHT SEE...

Angry Armadillo
This hard-shelled creature will nip an astronaut's ankle.

Yellow Billed Bird
Likes to dribble swamp water onto strangers.

Cave Dog
Lives in dark places and enjoys chewing robots.

Galactic Geek
Likes to sharpen its teeth on space buggies.

Ice Bird
Its feathers are as cold as snow. It has an icicle tail.

Plunger Nose
Harmless, unless it sniffs you, and then – watch out!

Beardy Bird
This friendly bird likes having splashy mud baths.

Mushroom Bird
If you touch the red spotted ones, you'll get an itchy rash.

Swamp Serpent
One will suck your socks, the other will chew your toes.

Answers

Pages 132-133 Getting ready
The six things Archie must take to Puzzle Planet are circled in red.

Pages 134-135 Star maze
The way through the star maze to Puzzle Planet is shown in red.

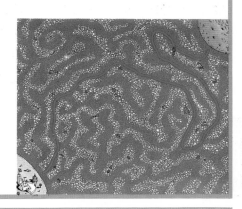

Pages 136-137 Space journey
Blip is here.

Pages 138-139 Planet puzzle
Archie has landed in a wild and scary part of Puzzle Planet.

Pages 140-141 Archie in trouble
The three friends in trouble are:

Betty from Blarg　　Victor the Vargon　　Pete from Planet Putty

Pages 142-143 Ice storm
Archie, Blip and the buggy can take shelter in this safe and empty cave.

Pages 144-145 Bubble trouble
This is the real Pete.

Pages 146-147 Spacey swamp
The route to Betty, and then to the other side of the swamp is shown in red.

Pages 148-149 Giant snails
The seven blue bananas are circled in red.

Pages 150-151 Following the signal

Archie has seen these switches and this microphone on page 140. They belong to Sydney.

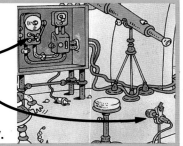

Pages 152-153 Trapped!

Sydney is standing on the teleporter.

Blip switches the teleporter on.

Sydney disappears to an unknown destination!

Pages 154-155 Canyon maze

This is Professor Moon's palace.

The way to it is shown in red.

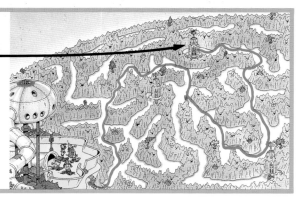

Pages 156-157 Just in time

The unexpected guest is Sydney!

His unknown destination was Professor Moon's palace.

Did you spot everything?

Space newts

Things to spot

Spy satellite

Remember that Archie must spot certain things once he arrives on Puzzle Planet. The chart below shows you how many space newts are hiding on each double page. You can also find out which of the Puzzle Planet objects is hidden where.

Did you remember to watch out for Sydney's spy satellite? Look back through the story and see if you can spot the satellite on each double page.

Pages	Space newts	Things to spot
136-137	three	star plant
138-139	three	bread fruit tree
140-141	two	green spider
142-143	one	footprint
144-145	five	Puzzle Planet flag
146-147	three	scaley goldfish
148-149	three	giant pink marshmallow
150-151	three	Puzzle Planet pencil
152-153	one	Puzzle Planet bug
154-155	one	red rock
156-157	five	friendly toffee apple

Something to think about

Although Sydney played some rather sneaky tricks on Archie and his friends, he did make it to Professor Moon's palace in the end. In fact, he was very well-behaved, and only had three helpings of Puzzle pop. Maybe next year it will be Sydney's turn to get his special badge, and be a real astronaut as well. What do you think?

PUZZLE MOUNTAIN

Contents

About this story

This story is about a brave mountain climber called Poppy Pickaxe, her pet puppy, Bernard, and their adventures on Puzzle Mountain. You will find a puzzle on every double page. See if you can solve them all. If you get stuck, you can look at the answers on pages 191 and 192.

Poppy Pickaxe

Bernard

The people of Puzzle Mountain are having a sports day. Poppy is especially excited because today she will try to climb to the very top of Puzzle Mountain.
Read this poster to find out more.

Puzzle Mountain

CALLING ALL BRAVE MOUNTAIN CLIMBERS!

Can you climb to the very top of Puzzle Mountain?
There is a prize for the first person to get there.

Mountain legend has it that the rare Yodel flower grows on top of Puzzle Mountain.
Take a photo of the flower to prove you've reached the top - but don't pick it!

Yodel flower
(artist's impression)

No one has ever reached the very top of Puzzle Mountain before. The way up is difficult and sometimes dangerous. Will Poppy be the first to make it?

Everyone entering the climbing competition must wear a hat with a red ribbon.

Things to spot.

The prizes for the sports day winners are missing. There is one prize hidden on every double page, except for pages 188 and 189. Look out for them. Here you can see all the prizes.

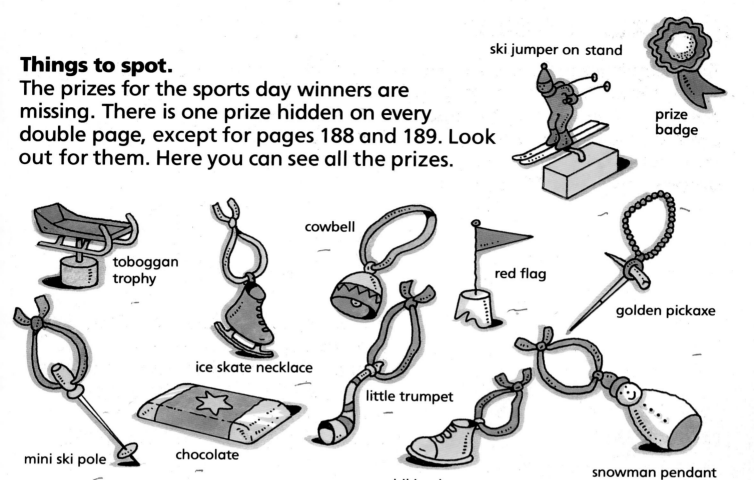

ski jumper on stand

prize badge

toboggan trophy

cowbell

red flag

golden pickaxe

ice skate necklace

little trumpet

mini ski pole

chocolate

hiking boot

snowman pendant

Basil

Basil collects rare mountain flowers. He wants to steal the Yodel flower. Watch out for him on every double page.

Mountain monster

People say that a strange, furry blue creature lives on Puzzle Mountain. Maybe you can spot him hiding on each double page.

Setting off

On the morning of her mountain climb, Poppy stepped out into the bustling village. High above her, far, far in the distance, loomed Puzzle Mountain.

Poppy wondered if the other climbers were as nervous as she was. Then she realized she didn't even know who they were. She remembered that everyone entering the climbing competition had to wear a red ribbon in their hat. Poppy looked around at all the people in the village. She soon spotted the other climbers.

Which path?

Poppy took one last look at the village. Then she called to Bernard, and the two friends bravely set off on their expedition.

Before long they arrived at six paths, all leading off in different directions. Only one path led right to the very peak of Puzzle Mountain. Poppy read the information board carefully. Then she looked at the signposts at the beginning of each path. She soon knew which one to take. She could even help the other hikers find their way.

Which path leads to the peak of Puzzle Mountain? Can you find the paths the others want?

Follow the signposts for:

HIKER'S HIGHWAY -

MOUNT LOFTY'S LANE -

WOODLAND WALK -

PUZZLE MOUNTAIN PEAK -

TRICKY TREK -

NUTTY NATURE TRAIL -

I'm looking for the Woodland Walk.

Which way to the Nutty Nature Trail?

Mountain musicians

Poppy bounded up the path. Soon she heard spluttering noises, and saw an old man trying to conduct a small band of musicians.

"Poppy!" he cried, turning around to face her. "These are the Puzzle Mountain musicians. They are trying to play their instruments, but they are making some very strange sounds."

Suddenly, as the old man spoke, the sound of music started behind him. He spun around. The musicians were now playing their instruments perfectly! The old man turned to Poppy again. He was mystified. What had happened? Poppy looked at the musicians and saw six simple changes that had made all the difference.

Can you spot the differences?

Lost goats

Poppy waved goodbye to the old man and his band and climbed on, further up the mountain path. After a while, she met her friend Gretel the goatherd. Gretel was crying.

"Oh Poppy," she wailed. "The music from those mountain musicians has frightened my goats away. I've lost all seven of them. Can you see them? They are all brown with white faces."

Can you find Gretel's seven lost goats?

Ice skating

Leaving the sound of bleating goats behind her, Poppy scrambled along the mountain path. The route was getting steeper, and the air was colder. The path passed by the Puzzle Mountain ice rink, where the skating competition was about to start. The ice was full of people, but four of the contestants looked very glum.

TICKETS

ICE SKATING COMPETITION TODAY

The girls' partners are boys, and the boys' partners are girls.

"Can you help us, Poppy?" they called. "Our skating partners are on the ice somewhere, but we can't find them with all these other people here. Our partners' outfits match our own."

Can you find the four missing skaters?

Food stop

Poppy left the ice skaters and began climbing again, up towards the top of Puzzle Mountain. Soon she came to a small restaurant.

"We've helped a lot of people, Bernard," she said. "It's time we had a treat. Let's get something nice to eat."

Bernard woofed in agreement, and the two friends went inside. There were so many delicious things for sale, they didn't know what to choose. They both wanted something to eat, and to drink, but they only had ten Puzzle Pennies to spend between them.

What can Poppy buy to eat and drink, and what can she buy for Bernard to eat and drink, with just ten Puzzle Pennies?

YUMMY CAKE – 8PP A SLICE

FRUIT – 4PP EACH

EGGS – 4PP EACH

JUICE 3PP A GLASS

CAKE – 5PP A SLICE

PASTRIES 2PP EACH

TASTY ROLLS – 3PP EACH

CAKE – 6PP A SLICE

DELUXE DRINK – 7PP A GLASS

SOUP – 6PP A BOWL

PEOPLE FOOD

Ski lift

Poppy licked the crumbs from her lips, and left the restaurant. She set off up the path once more, but stopped when she saw a group of eight grumpy looking skiers.

"We've got to take this ski lift to the other side of the mountain," grumbled the smallest skier. "But this notice has really confused us. Which chairs should each one of us use?"

"Everyone needs help today," thought Poppy as she read the big notice board.

Do you know which skier should use which chair?

Please read instructions before taking lift:

BLUE CHAIR - two adults only

RED CHAIR - one very tall person only

GREEN CHAIR - two adults with hats only

YELLOW CHAIR - cannot hold much weight

PURPLE CHAIR - two children only

RESTAURANT

We always travel together.

Sorting the skis

Poppy couldn't take the ski lift. She had to continue on the mountain path. She puffed and panted her way up. Before long, she bumped into her friend Tim, who was looking at a line of skis stuck into the snow.

"I am in the skiing competition today," he said. "But I can't find my speedy racing skis. I know they are the only matching pair here."

Can you find Tim's matching skis?

Toboggan race

Dodging the skiers, Poppy pressed on. A little higher up the mountain, she came across a toboggan race that was just about to start. The team that finished the course in the fastest time would be the winner. The three toboggan teams thought the course was very easy, but Poppy wasn't so sure.

"Be careful," she warned. "There are plenty of obstacles and dead ends along the way. Look out for them."

Can you find the clear route from the start to the finish of the race?

Ice walk

Poppy waved goodbye to the toboggan teams and carried on, climbing higher and higher up Puzzle Mountain. Soon there were no more people around, the mist was coming down, and Poppy and Bernard were on their own. They slid across the slippery ground. As they turned a corner, they stopped and gasped.

In front of them was the strangest glacier Poppy had ever seen. Beyond it, towered the very top of Puzzle Mountain. They were nearly there! But first they had to cross the ice, avoiding the deep pools and broken planks. There were two large notices on the glacier. Poppy peered at them through her blizzard-proof binoculars.

To get safely across the glacier, feed the wild snow bears with the six ice cream cones you'll find on the way.

Watch out for WOLVES. They don't eat ice cream.

She couldn't quite believe what she read. Wild snow bears and wolves? She hadn't expected this at all. It was going to be a dangerous journey...

Can you find the safe route across the glacier, picking up the six ice cream cones as you go?

Nearly there

Poppy skidded and slithered across the last of the ice. She landed with a crunch on the snowy bank on the other side of the glacier. Looking up ahead, she could see the peak of Puzzle Mountain, poking through the cloudy mist.

"Follow me, Bernard," she said. And the two friends began the final climb, upward and onward.

The way up was steep and very dangerous.

They hid from huge snowballs.

The air got thinner, and it was difficult to breathe. But at last the mist began to clear...

Poppy was amazed to see spikes of ice rising out of the mountain. Even more surprising were the holes, almost like windows, carved into the icy spikes. Then she spotted something she had only seen a picture of before. She had reached the very top of Puzzle Mountain.

What has Poppy spotted?

Mountain monsters

Click! Poppy took a photo of the Yodel flower. All at once, a huge hairy hand grabbed her arm and pulled her backwards. Poppy blinked, and in a flash she realized she was standing inside a room in a strange ice house. Three blue creatures were looking at her. Poppy rubbed her eyes. She was staring at a family of Puzzle Mountain monsters! Just then, a smaller monster rushed into the room and began to speak.

"I'm sorry I scared you Poppy," said the biggest monster. "But I am the guardian of the Yodel flower and I must protect it. It is the only one in the world, you know. Now I expect you want to get back to the sports day celebrations. Take my super-speedy red toboggan. It will get you down the mountain in no time – if I can find it."

Where is the super-speedy red toboggan?

Poppy returns

Night was falling as Poppy clambered on board the super-speedy red toboggan. She waved goodbye to her new friends, and with a whoosh she and Bernard were off, whizzing down the other side of Puzzle Mountain. As they sped on, Poppy caught a glimpse of Basil, looking very scared. Perhaps now he would think twice before stealing any more mountain flowers.

Can you spot Basil?
Who is scaring him?

Did you spot?

Poppy reached the top of Puzzle Mountain first, and won a golden pickaxe! But whatever happened to the other eight competitors? How far did they get?

Below, you can see pictures of the other climbers, and read a little more about them. Now look back carefully through the story and see if you can spot them all.

Lady Cicily
She is clumsy, and rather accident prone.

Hungry Harry
He is always hungry and eats anything and everything.

Fred Photo
He likes mountain climbing – and photography.

Friendly Flora
She likes to stop and chat with her friends.

Lazy Larry
The fresh mountain air may make this sleepy climber drowsy.

Daredevil Dot
Her daredevil activities can be dangerous.

Fisher Jim
He enjoys climbing, but sometimes he'd rather be fishing.

Katy Climber
She wears baggy trousers, which may trip her up.

Answers

Pages 164-165 Setting off
The other mountain climbers are circled in red.

Pages 166-167 Which path?
Puzzle Mountain Peak

Nutty Nature Trail

Woodland Walk

Pages 168-169 Mountain musicians
The differences are circled in red.
Can you find the extra differences?

Pages 170-171 Lost goats
The seven missing goats are circled in red.

Pages 172-173 Ice skating
The missing skating partners are circled in red.

Pages 174-175 Food stop
Poppy buys a pastry for two Puzzle Pennies, and a glass of juice for three Puzzle Pennies. For Bernard she buys a tasty bone for two Puzzle Pennies, and a bowl of doggy drink, for three Puzzle Pennies. This adds up to ten Puzzle Pennies exactly.

Pages 176-177 Ski lift

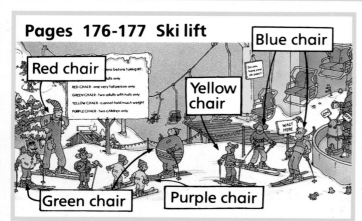

Red chair

Blue chair

Yellow chair

Green chair

Purple chair

Pages 178-179 Sorting the skis
These are Tim's matching skis.

These are his poles.

191

Pages 180-181 Toboggan race

The clear route from the start to the finish of the race is shown in red.

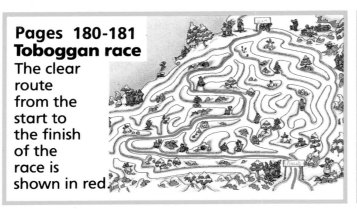

Pages 182-183 Ice walk

The six ice cream cones are circled in red. The safe route across the glacier is shown in black.

Pages 184-185 Nearly there

Poppy has spotted the Yodel flower.

Pages 186-187 Mountain monsters

The super-speedy red toboggan is here.

Pages 188-189 Poppy returns

The monster is scaring Basil!

Did you spot everything?

Sports day prizes

The chart below shows you which sports day prize is hidden on which double page.

Basil

Puzzle Mountain monster

Basil and the monster

Did you remember to watch out for Basil, and for the Puzzle Mountain monster? Look back through the story and see if you can spot them on each double page.

Pages	Prize
164-165	hiking boot
166-167	little trumpet
168-169	cowbell
170-171	ice skate necklace
172-173	chocolate
174-175	ski jumper on stand
176-177	mini ski pole
178-179	toboggan trophy
180-181	red flag
182-183	snowman pendant
184-185	prize badge
186-187	golden pickaxe

First published in 1993 by Usborne Publishing Ltd., Usborne House, 83-85 Saffron Hill, London EC1N 8RT, England.

Copyright © 1993 Usborne Publishing Ltd.

The name Usborne and the device ♛ are Trade Marks of Usborne Publishing Ltd.

Printed in Portugal. UE